THE REMAINING

STORY BY:
CASEY LA SCALA
SCREENPLAY BY:
CASEY LA SCALA AND CHRIS DOWLING
ADAPTATION BY:
ROLAND MANN
EDITED BY:
KELLY AYRIS
DESIGN & PACKAGE BY:
ZACH MATHENY, KEN RANEY

PENCILS BY:
KYLE HOTZ
INKS BY:
ERIC LAYTON, JASON MOORE, JOHN BEATTY, JOSEF RUBINSTEIN
COLORS BY:
EMILY KANALZ
LETTERS BY:
ZACH MATHENY

Published by Kingstone Comics
www.KingstoneMedia.com
Copyright © 2014

Printed in USA

Kingstone Comics

No part of this publication may be reproduced, stored in a retrieval system or transmitted in any form by any means, electronic, mechanical, photo copy, recording or otherwise, without the prior permission of the publisher, except as provided by United States copyright law.

AND LAST.

MY LAST, DAD! PROMISE!

PLEASE RAISE YOUR GLASSES HIGH AND WISH MY BEST FRIEND, SKYLAR, AND HER AMAZING HUSBAND, DAN, A FULFILLING AND PROSPEROUS FUTURE TOGETHER.

CAKE FOR THE GIRL AT TABLE ONE?

IS IT DIET?

THE WEDDING'S OVER. YOU CAN QUIT STARVING YOURSELF.

GOOD POINT.

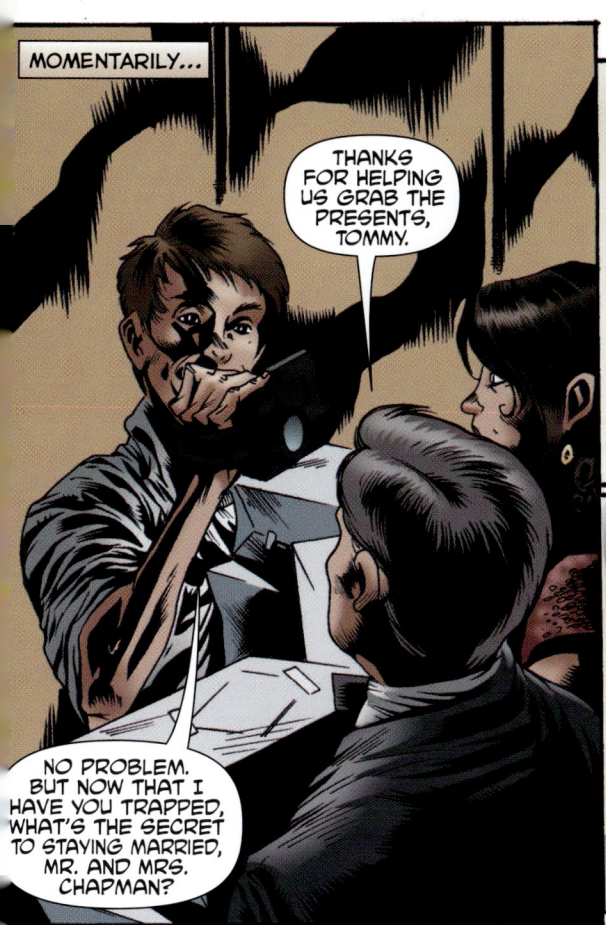

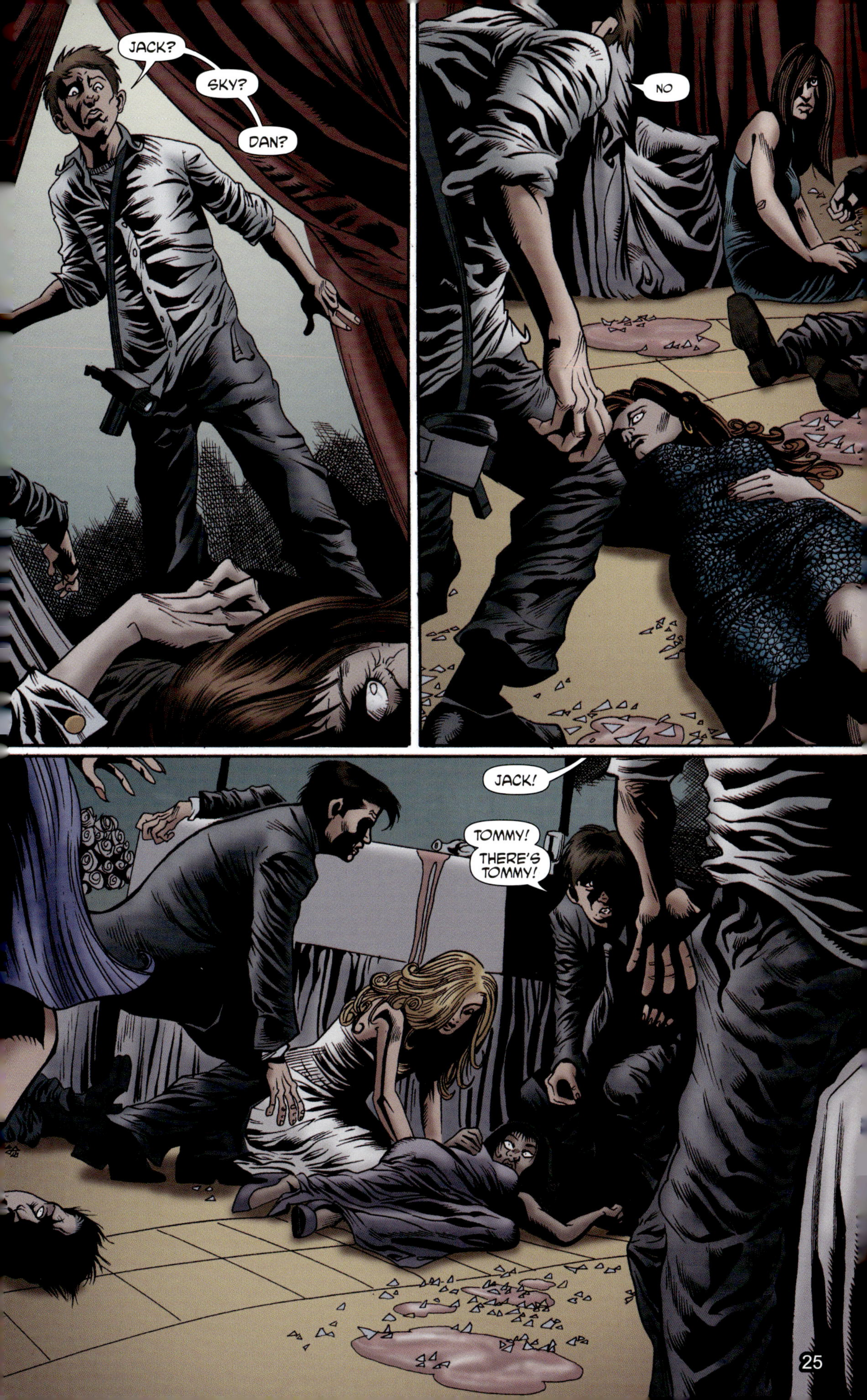

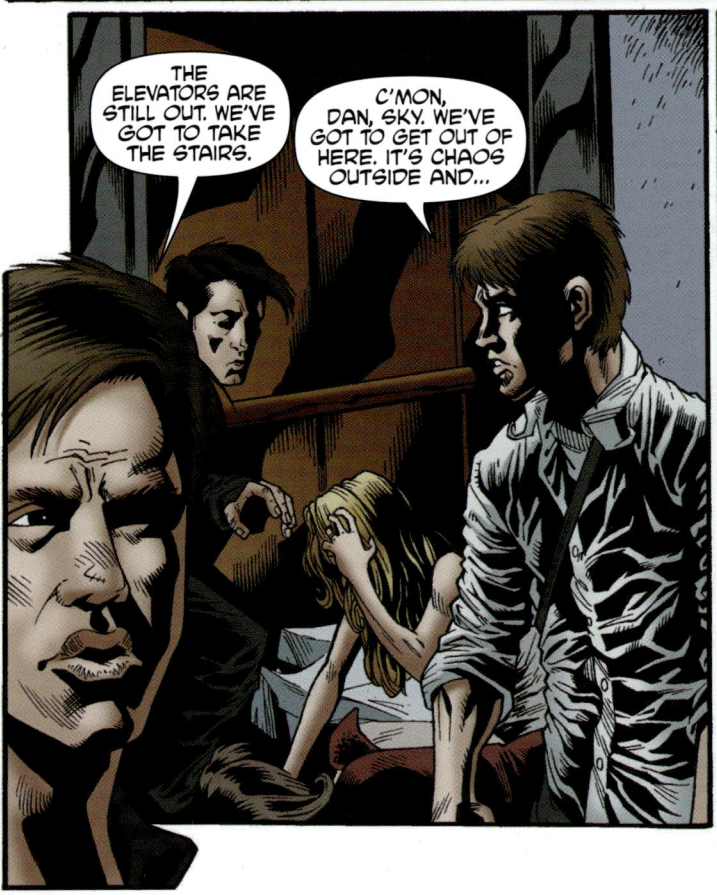

...WE'RE COMING WITH YOU.

C'MON THEN, LET'S TAKE THE SIDE EXIT.

WE CAN'T RISK BEING NEAR THOSE BIG WINDOWS.

LET'S GO!

WHAT THE...?

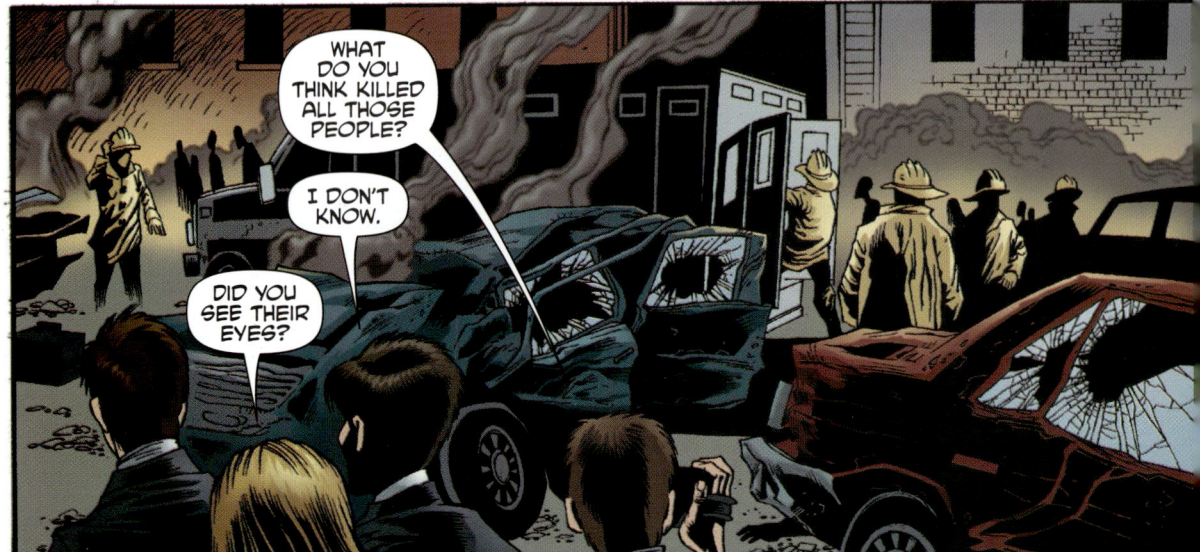

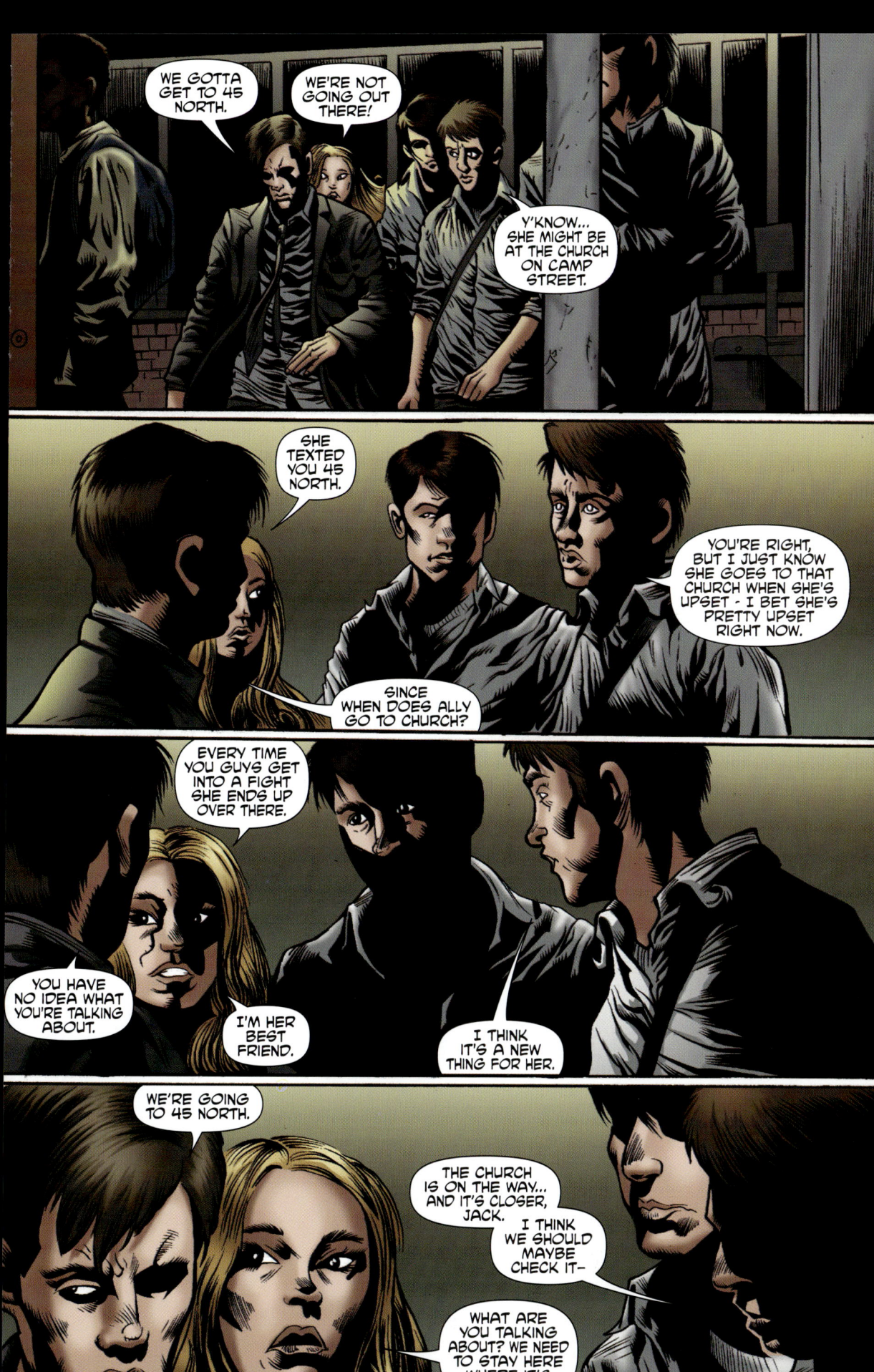

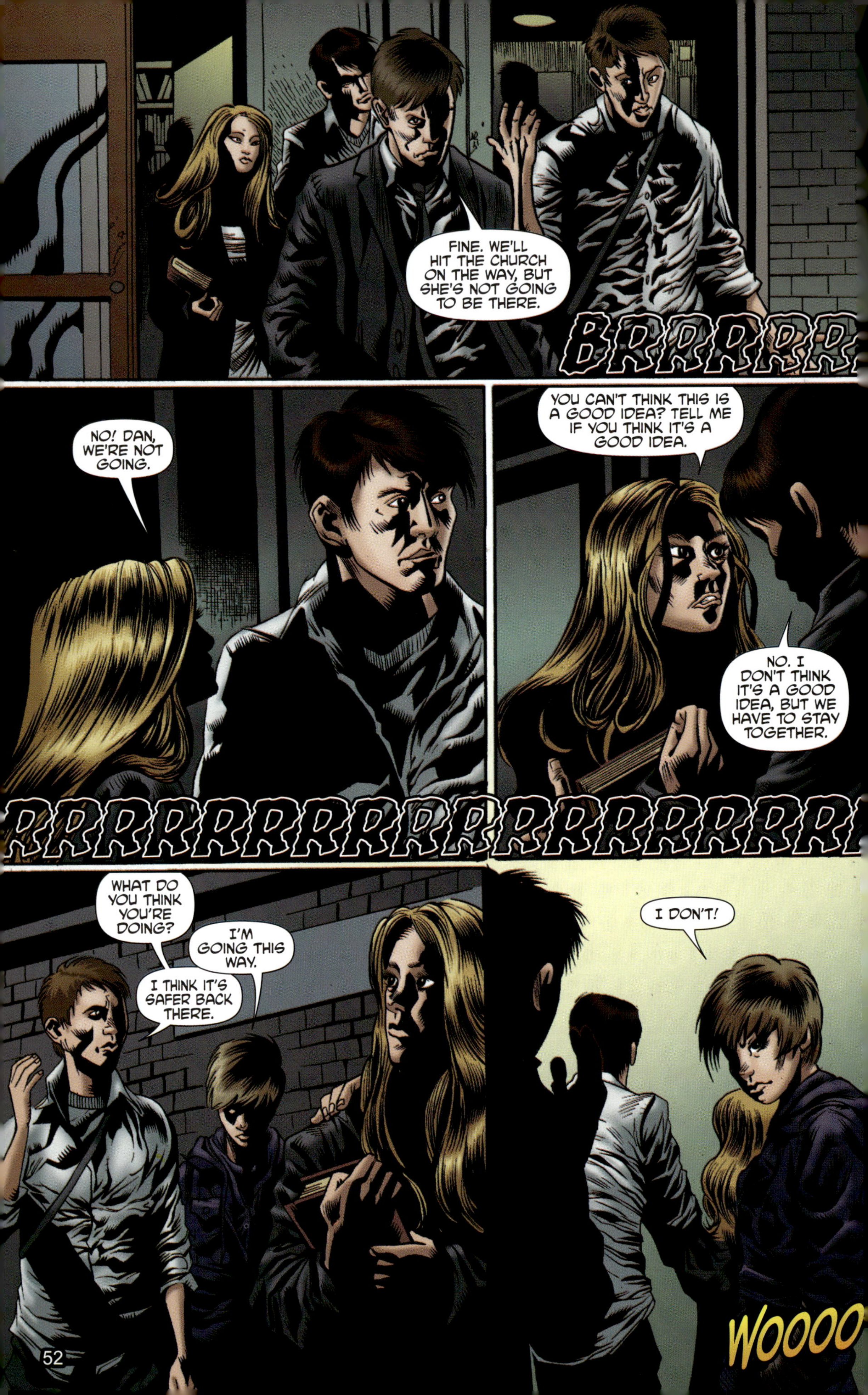

FINE. WE'LL HIT THE CHURCH ON THE WAY, BUT SHE'S NOT GOING TO BE THERE.

BRRRRR

NO! DAN, WE'RE NOT GOING.

YOU CAN'T THINK THIS IS A GOOD IDEA? TELL ME IF YOU THINK IT'S A GOOD IDEA.

NO. I DON'T THINK IT'S A GOOD IDEA, BUT WE HAVE TO STAY TOGETHER.

RRRRRRRRRRRRRRRRRRRR

WHAT DO YOU THINK YOU'RE DOING?

I'M GOING THIS WAY.

I THINK IT'S SAFER BACK THERE.

I DON'T!

WOOOO

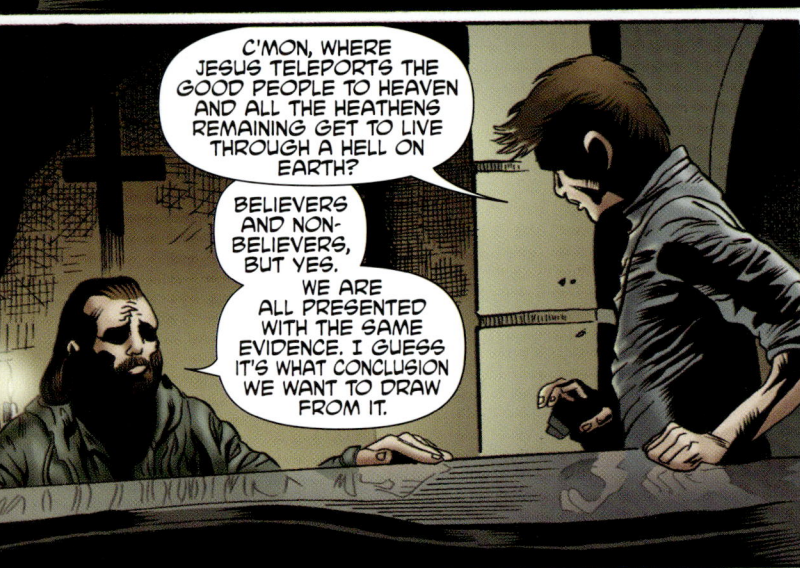

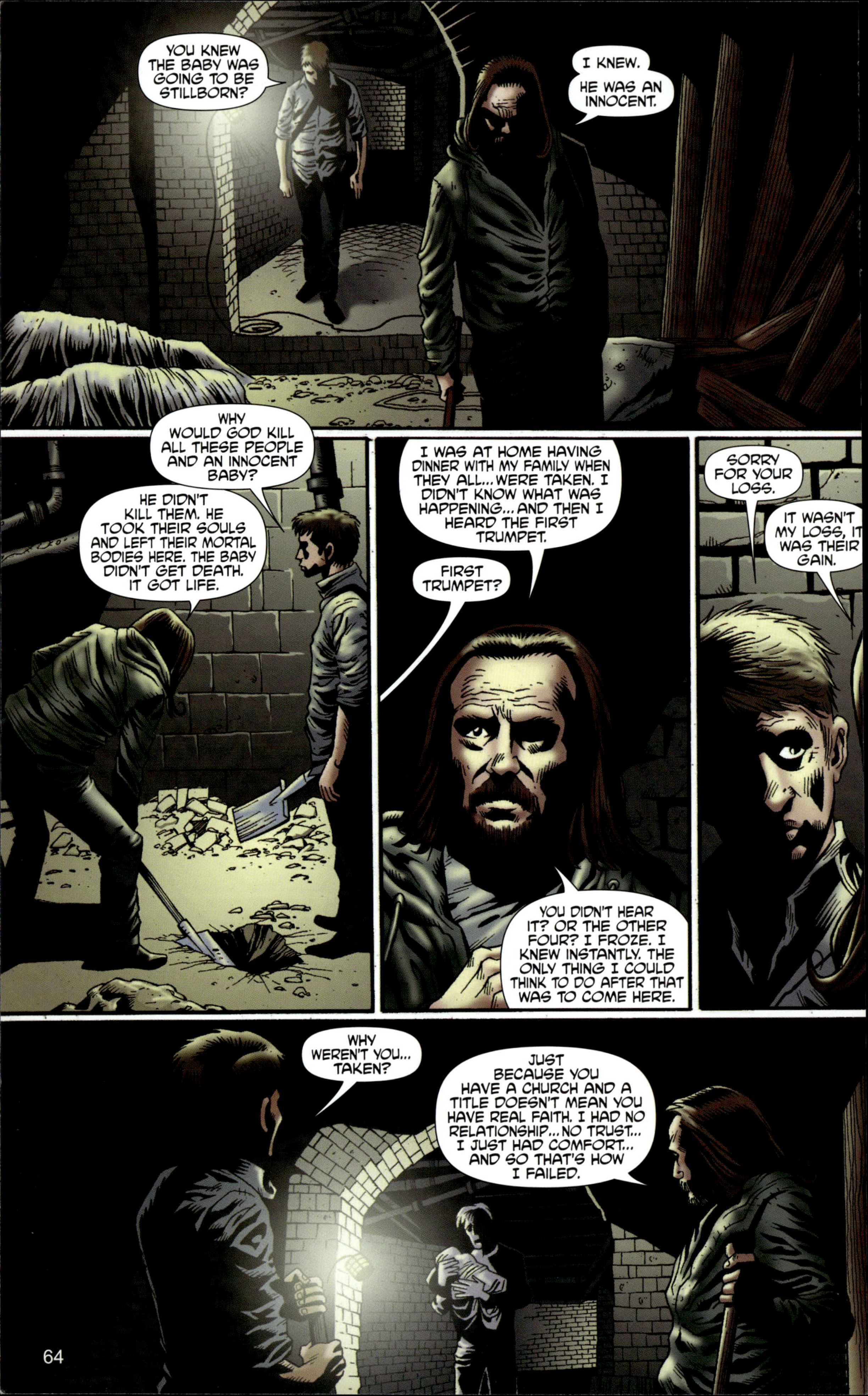

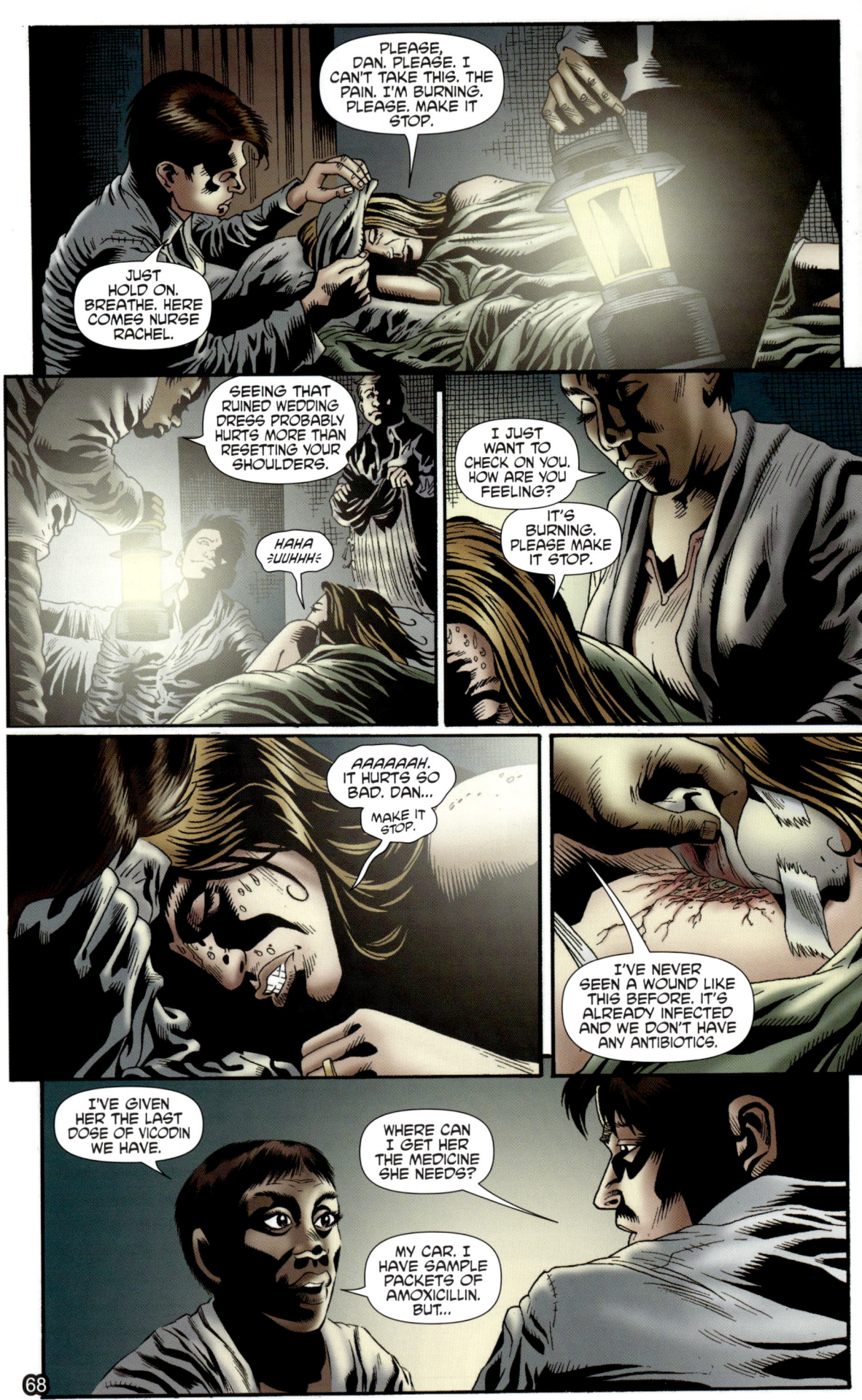

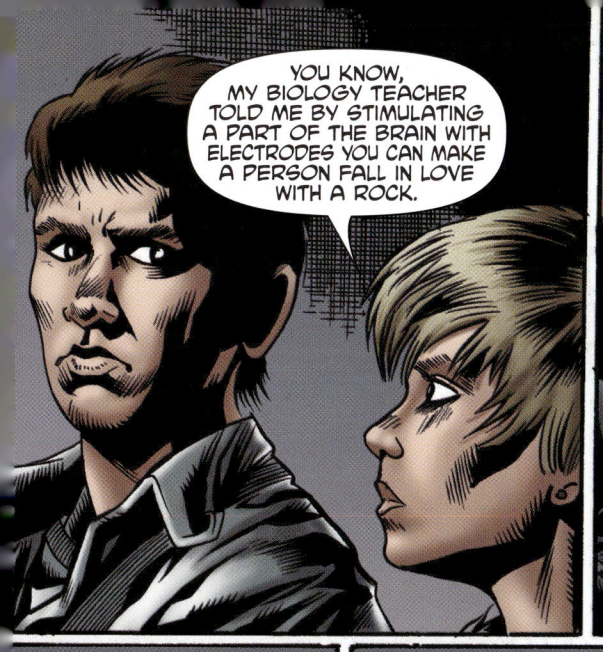

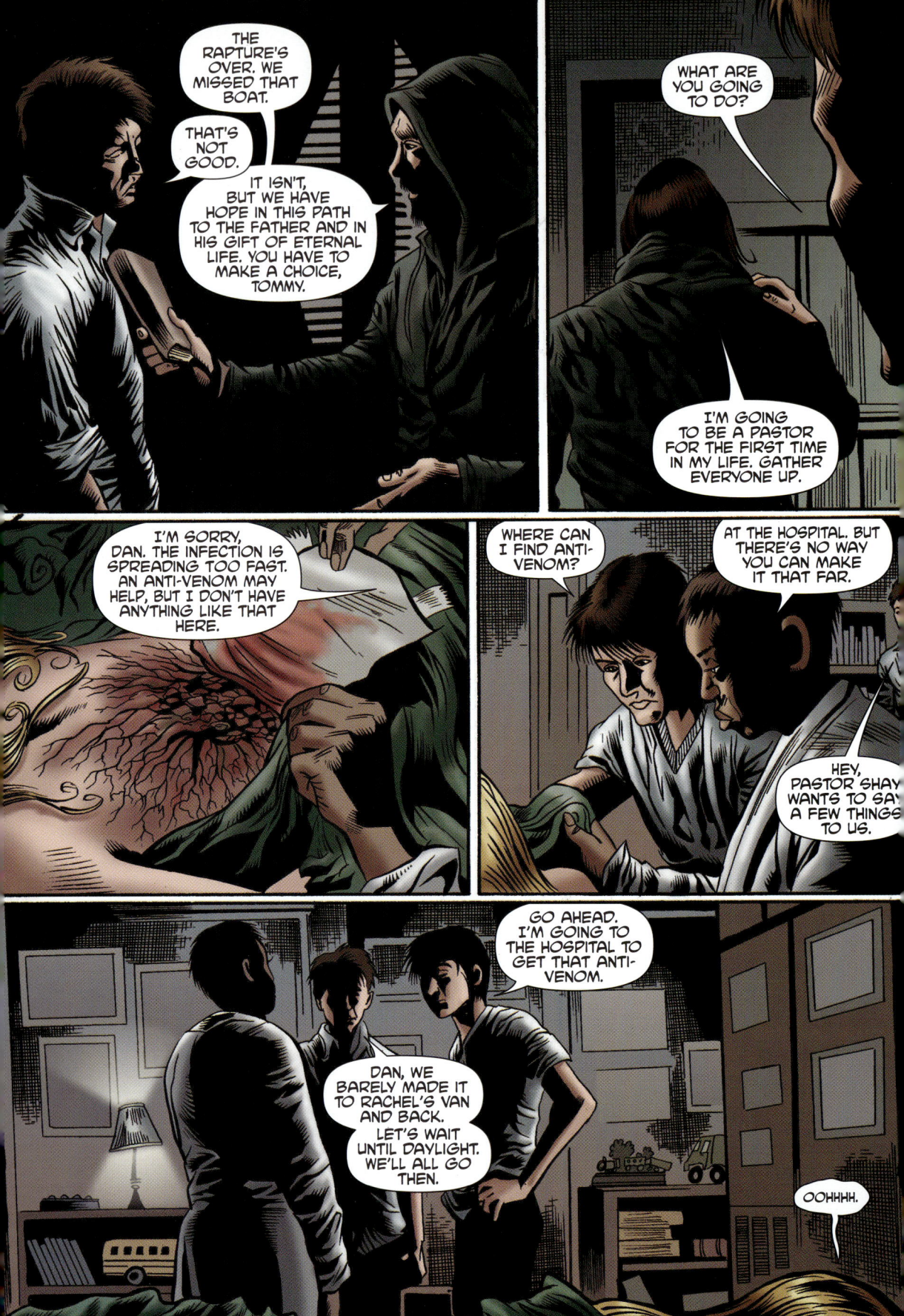

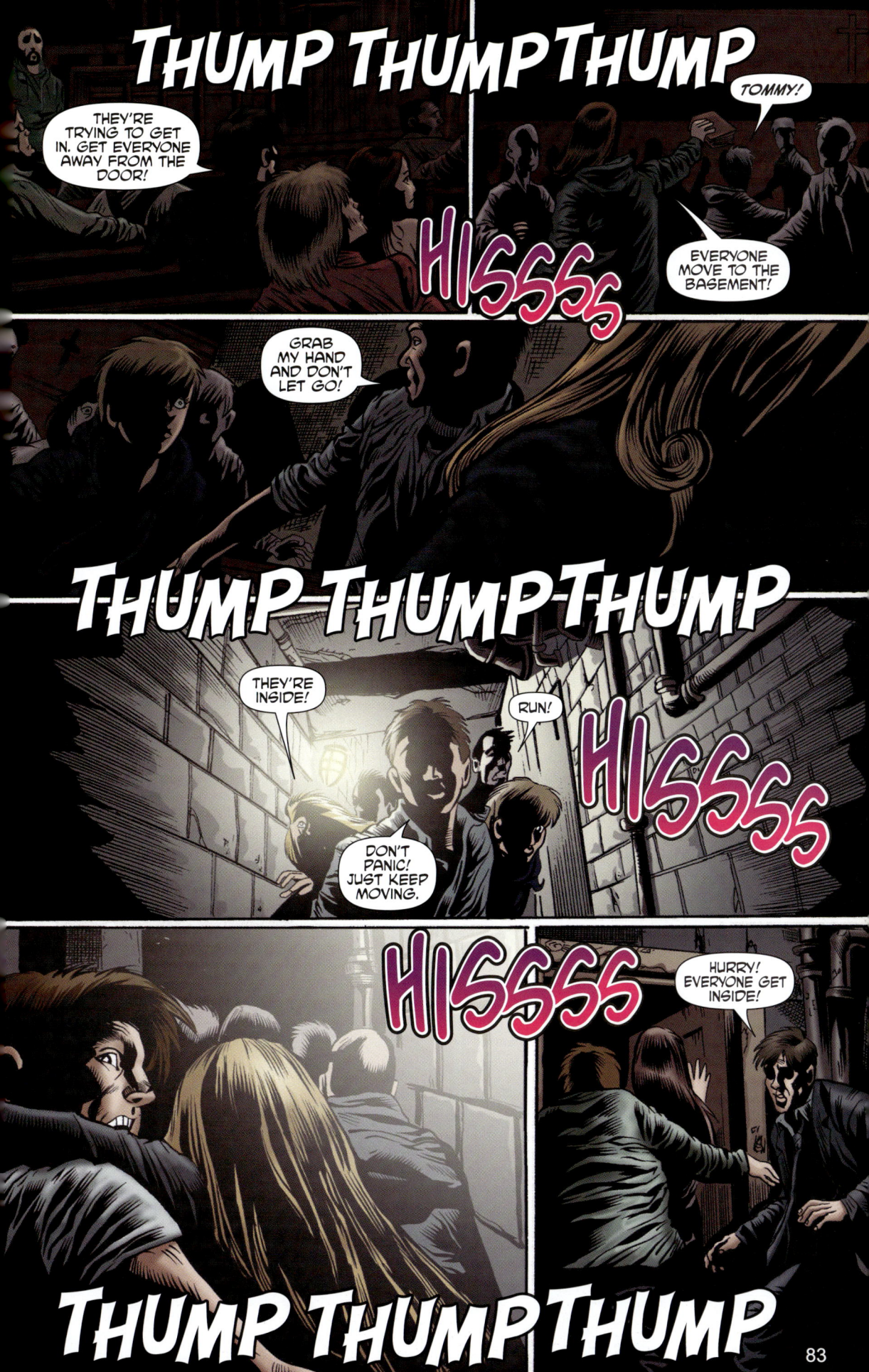

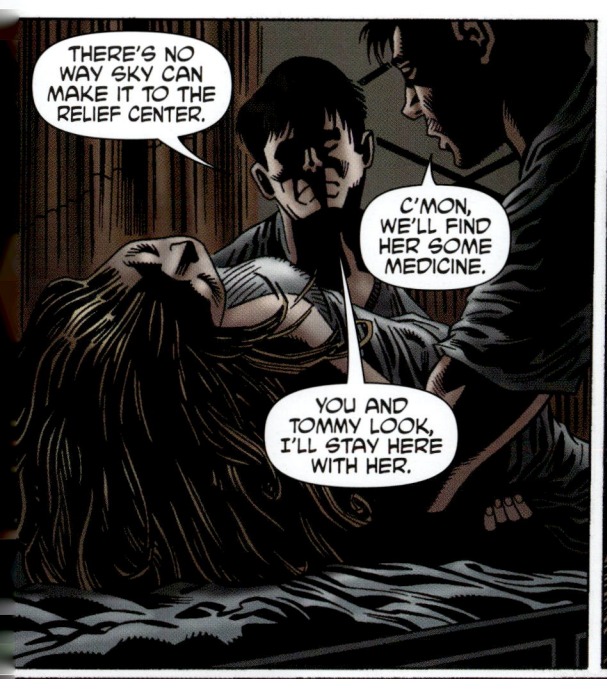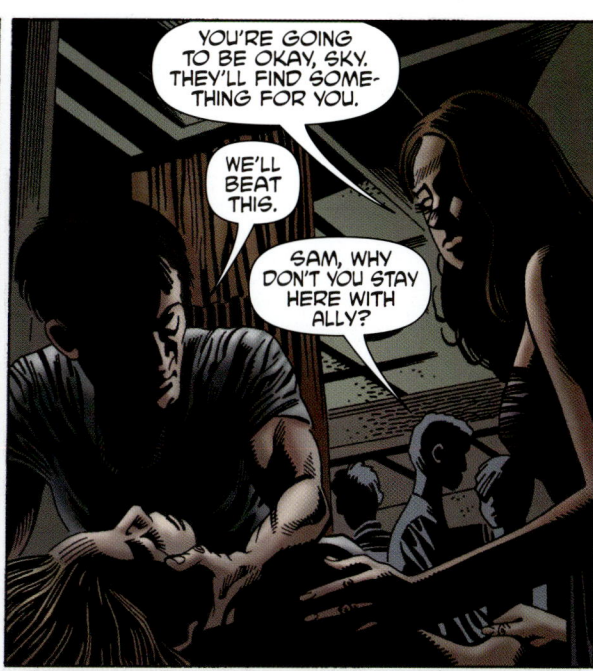

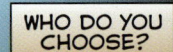